The Two Brothers

Alexandre Dumas

Translated and Adapted By:
Nathan Dickmeyer

Illustrated By:
Roya Sadeghi

Bahar Books
www.baharbooks.com

Dumas, Alexandre
The Two Brothers (Translated from French)/Alexandre Dumas

Adapted and Translated by: Nathan Dickmeyer

Translated from *Collection Motifs n° 315,* Group Privat/Le Rocher, 2008.

Illustrated By: Roya Sadeghi

ISBN-10: 1939099390
ISBN-13: 978-1-939099-39-6

Translator's Introduction

The Two Brothers is based on an Alexandre Dumas (père) fairy tale written during one of the two periods in which he wrote stories for children: 1832 to 1844 and 1852 to 1860. Between these two periods he wrote his great romantic novels, including *The Three Musketeers (1844)*. In 1838 Dumas took a trip down the Rhine, absorbing the wondrous folk tales of that region, many of which live today in Wagner's operas. In 1839 he published *The Adventures of Lyderic*, which was packaged with *The Two Brothers* and published in 2008 by Groupe Privat/Le Rocher in their Collection Motifs as *Motifs no. 315*.

In *The Two Brothers* Dumas creates several magical scenes where five different animals talk and do the bidding of the brothers. In these episodes each animal repeats a phrase or action in a way that is delightfully childlike. The tale develops the moral strengths of brotherhood, perseverance, patience, truth, courage, and faithfulness. The loyalty and fellowship of the five animals, all natural enemies, echoes and reinforces the story's moral themes. Each brother and his animals becomes a family, where the clash of characters is both colorful and a source of strength.

Unfortunately, Dumas spills out his original story a bit too recklessly. Characters get lost. One brother nearly disappears from the tale completely and never develops an independent persona. Out of all the characters, only two of the animals develop real voices: the lion and the rabbit. Dumas also violates some of the unwritten rules of fairy tales: dragons should never be hunted with guns, and birds of pure gold should never be killed and roasted.

After my initial translation of the tale, I discussed the story with the mother of my principal audience, Ethan, a bright Chinese-American seven year old. I was told that Ethan would find the killing of a dragon reprehensible and that the great scenes of violence and murder, including the drawing and quartering of the primary evil-doer and the burning of the witch, would simply not be acceptable in a modern home, especially one with Chinese cultural roots.

There is also a strong Christian undercurrent in this story. At first, I wanted to work my way around it, but that would be dishonest. The particular articles of faith are less important than the role of faith itself. It would be disingenuous of me to declare that I live above faith. My faith in love is as strong as Gottlieb's faith in St. Hubert. While this adaptation is gentler than Dumas's original, it does not lose the moral lessons he wished to impart. Acts of kindness are repaid, patience is greatly rewarded, and strength of character is the mark of heroes.

Nathan Dickmeyer

For Ethan

— N. D.

ჰ

Once, a long, long time ago, there were two brothers: one rich and the other poor.

The one who was rich was a goldsmith and had a heart as hard as the touchstone he used to test his gold.

The other was poor and lived by making brooms. He was good and honest.

The poor one had two children, two boys; the rich one had none.

The two young boys were twins and resembled each other so much that their parents had to make tiny marks on their ears to tell them apart.

The two boys had lost their mother when they were young and often came to their uncle's house, but rarely would they be allowed even a crumb from his table.

Now it happened that the poor brother, going one day to the wood to look for broomstraw, saw a bird of gold more beautiful than anything he had ever seen. He picked up a stone and threw it and hit the bird.

But because the bird was just taking flight, he only hit the tip of a wing and just a single feather fell. This feather, nonetheless, was pure gold.

The poor broom-maker picked it up and carried it to the home of his brother, who examined it, tested it with his touchstone, and said: "This is pure, unalloyed gold," and gave his brother a bag of silver for the feather.

The next day, the poor brother climbed a silver birch to cut some branches and saw there the same bird that he had seen the day before, taking off a second time.

He searched the tree carefully and found its nest, which contained an egg of gold, just like the bird itself.

He carried this egg to his brother's house and showed it to him, and the goldsmith said again: "This is pure, unalloyed gold," and gave his brother the exact fair value of silver for it, saying this time, "I would very much like to have the bird itself. I will give you a very good price for it."

The next day the poor brother returned to the wood and covered himself with silver birch leaves and twigs. He then climbed the silver birch of the bird of gold and, after making a small opening in the bottom of the nest, hid beneath it.

When the bird of gold returned to her nest, he reached through the hole and seized her by a leg. As he ran with her to his brother, the nest still around his arm, she cried, "Release me and you will be rewarded," but he held her tight.

"Well, well!" said the brother. "Here is the bird just as I asked," and the goldsmith gave his brother twenty pieces of gold and shoved the poor bird into a small wooden cage that hung in his kitchen.

1

The poor broom-seller returned home full of joy. He had enough money now to live for an entire year, not having to make a single broom.

Now, the goldsmith was learned and crafty. He knew the legend of the bird of gold. He called to his wife and said, "Roast this bird for me so carefully that nothing is lost. I must eat the whole thing, and I must eat it all by myself, alone!"

This bird, as you undoubtedly knew, was not an ordinary fowl, and anyone who ate its liver and its heart was certain to find two pieces of gold under his pillow each morning when he awoke.

Now, it just so happened that, while the oven was warming and the goldsmith's wife was obliged to run an absolutely necessary errand, the broom-maker's two boys came into their uncle's kitchen. The bird of gold rattled her cage and cried softly, "Release me."

The brother who was born first by barely a minute, and who was therefore older, climbed onto a chair and from there climbed to the table. The younger brother followed his brother onto the table and the two stared up at the beautiful bird and felt very sad. Then the younger said, "Let me climb on your back. I will lift the latch." He then climbed up and released the bird.

Just at that moment, the wife returned and saw the bird fleeing.

"What have you done?" she demanded.

And so that her husband would not guess what had happened, she killed a large pigeon and made a sauce with the goldsmith's golden egg.

When the bird was done, she carried it to the goldsmith who ate the entire thing without leaving anything, but the next morning when he inspected his pillow, looking for the two pieces of gold, to his great astonishment, he found nothing there out of the ordinary.

As for the two children, they knew nothing of the good luck they shared, but when they got up the morning after, some objects fell ringing to the ground.

They gathered up what had fallen and found they had two pieces of gold.

They took the pieces of gold to their father, who was astonished. "How did this happen?" he asked.

But when, the next morning, they again found two pieces of gold, then again the following morning, and the morning following that, and again each morning after, the seller of brooms went looking for the goldsmith and told him this strange story.

The goldsmith immediately realized how this had happened and that the children had released the bird and his reward had been bestowed on them instead

And, for revenge and because he was jealous and cruel, he said to the father: "Your children are in league with the devil. This gold will bring you harm. Do not allow them to remain any longer in your home. After taking them, the devil might take you as well."

"But what do you think I should do with these poor innocent children, brother?" said he to the goldsmith.

"Lose them in the forest. If the devil has nothing to do with them, God will protect them. If, on the contrary, they belong to the devil, what can we do? They will have to settle their business with him."

Even though it made him deeply sad, the poor broom-seller tried to follow the goldsmith's advice.

He led the children into the wood, and where the trees of the forest were thickest, he left them, intending to return after, perhaps, the devil had been frightened out of them.

He hid behind a silver birch. Suddenly he saw the bird of gold and ran after it. He ran and ran. Finally, the bird just disappeared into the golden haze of the setting sun, and he could not find his way back to his children. He returned to his home, broken-hearted.

When the children realized that their father had gone on without them, they tried to find their way home, but they were entirely lost.

The more they walked, the more deeply into the forest they went.

They walked all night, calling and crying, but the only responses they got were the howls of the wolves, the barks of the foxes, and the cries of the wildcats.

2

Finally, the next morning they encountered a hunter, who asked them, "To whom do you belong, my children?"

"Alas, sir," they replied, "we are the sons of a poor broom-maker who does not wish to keep us because we find each morning, my brother and I, a piece of gold under our pillow."

"Well!" said the hunter. "It seems to me that there is nothing very bad about that, but only if you remain always honest and do not allow these gold pieces to turn the two of you into lazy fellows."

"Sir," said the two children, "we are honest and we do not ask for anything more than to work."

"Ah well, come with me," said the good man. "I shall be your father and will raise you."

And since he had no children himself, he took them into his home and sought to fulfill the promise he had made.

He began taking them hunting with him, and in time, they became the finest archers in the entire district.

Not only that, but every morning, each of the two youths found a piece of gold under his pillow, and the hunter carefully put each piece aside so that someday, should they have the need, each could reclaim his small treasure.

One day, when they had grown and their reputations as hunters were made, their adoptive father brought them with him to the wood. "Today," said he, "you will each prove to me that your aim is true. I will then know that you are true hunters, and you will have ended your apprenticeship."

They then went together to where they were hidden. They waited a long while, but no game appeared. Then the old hunter looked up and saw a large flock of wild geese flying in a wedge.

"Now," said he to the eldest whose name was Wilfred, "hit the geese that fly at each end of the wedge."

Wilfred notched two arrows in his bow, aimed quickly and let them fly, hitting the two geese indicated by his adoptive father.

He had won his place as a true hunter.

An instant later, another flock of geese appeared. These flew in a single line.

"It is your turn," said their adoptive father to the younger who was named Gottlieb, "take the first and last of these geese."

And Gottlieb notched, pulled, aimed and released two arrows and each hit one of the designated geese.

He had also won his place as a true hunter.

Their adoptive father said to the two brothers, "You have ended your apprenticeship as hunters. You are free."

The two young men then stepped a little away from their adoptive father and exchanged a few words in low voices. Then they returned home with the old hunter.

But when night had fallen, and they were called to supper, Wilfred, speaking for himself and his brother, said to the old hunter, "Father, we will not touch one bit of this food until you agree to one request."

"And what is this request?" said the old hunter.

Wilfred responded, "It is that, as you have said, we have completed our apprenticeship as hunters, and we now wish to see the world. Allow us, therefore, my brother and me, to leave and go our way."

As soon as the old hunter heard these words, he cried joyously, "You speak like true hunters. Your wish has always been mine as well. Go out into the world. I see happiness coming to both of you."

Then with great joy they drank and ate.

3

When the day set for their departure arrived, the old hunter gave each of his adopted sons a beautiful bow laminated of seven woods and a silver arrow and said to them to take from their treasure as many pieces of gold as they wished.

Then he walked with them along the road. Arriving at the spot where they had decided to part, he gave them, before taking his leave, a beautiful knife. Its blade was brilliant and unmarked, and he said to them, "If you become separated one day, my dear children, bury the point of this knife in a tree at the spot where your roads part. And when one of you returns to this road, that one will be able to see how things have gone for his brother, because if one of you dies, the side of the blade turned toward the road which that one followed will be completely rusted, while the other side toward the road of the living brother will remain pure and bright."

Wilfred took the knife. Then both of them embraced their adoptive father and continued on their way.

That evening, they came to a forest so large that they could not even think of crossing it in one day. They sat down at the foot of a tree, ate what they had brought with them in their sacks and slept under the beautiful stars.

The next day they again set off. That evening, when they had to stop for the day, they still had not reached the far edge of the forest. This time, however, their sacks were empty and one said to the other, "We must kill an animal to feed ourselves or else we will spend a very bad night here."

He notched an arrow and began kicking through the underbrush, making a rabbit run out. He pulled the bowstring to his cheek and was about to shoot, when the rabbit cried, "My dear hunter, let me live, and I will give you two young rabbits."

This seemed like trading dinner for its shadow, but the young man took the word of the rabbit, who re-entered the wood and an instant later, in fact, produced two little rabbits.

But they were so gentle and played so tenderly with each other that the hunters could not kill them. The brothers kept them near and the young rabbits understood to follow them, walking at their heels like two spaniels.

Nevertheless, they had to eat, and, although the two young men had calmed their hunger a little with some sweet acorns, when they scared up a fox, one of them notched an arrow and pulled his bowstring to his cheek.

But the fox cried, "Oh! My dear hunter, let me live, and I will give you two kit foxes."

The hunter thought that two young foxes would be better to eat than one old fox. He made a sign to the fox and lowered his bow, consenting to the exchange. An instant later, the fox brought him two little ones.

But just as they were about to shoot the kits, the two young hunters lost heart, and they made them the companions of the rabbits and for supper, contented themselves with some chestnuts that had fallen under a tree.

Then they promised themselves that they would shoot the first animal they encountered.

The first animal was a wolf.

The two young men were just about to kill it when the wolf cried, "Oh! My dear hunters, let me live and I will give you two young wolves."

The two young men accepted the exchange, and the two young wolves were made deputies of the two little rabbits and the two little foxes who were already following them.

They next came upon a bear, who, seeing herself threatened, hastily cried, as had the others, "Oh! My dear hunters, let me live and I will give you two bear cubs."

The two bear cubs were brought and put with the other animals and as they were not only the strongest, but had a grand and thoughtful air, they were charged by the young men to keep watch over the others.

They had barely finished these arrangements, and the young bears were taking up their posts, when a lion came toward them roaring and shaking his mane. But the two hunters were not frightened by this menace and drew back their bowstrings, when the lion, seeing that the two meant business, cried, "My dear hunters, let me live, and I will give you two young lions."

And the lion delivered two young lions, such that the hunters had two lions, two bears, two wolves, two foxes and two rabbits who followed them and served them.

Only finding very little to eat in this forest and becoming hungrier and hungrier, they said to the two foxes, "You two who are so clever and cunning, can you get us something to eat?"

The foxes talked this over between them and then gave this advice: "Very near here," they said, "there is a village where our father and our mother found chickens to bring to us. We will show you the way."

The foxes then showed the road to the village to the two brothers. There they bought something to eat for themselves and also a bit of food to give their beasts. Then they went on their way.

In this region the foxes knew where to find a good many chicken houses for the young hunters, who, from then on, thanks to the foxes, never suffered from hunger.

They continued traveling for some time, offering their services to the large landowners whose chateaus lay along their route. But everywhere they went they were told, "We could use a hunter, but not two."

They knew then that they must separate.

They divided up the animals such that each had a lion, a bear, a wolf, a fox, and a rabbit. Then, they said goodbye, swearing brotherly devotion until death.

Before separating, they planted the knife that they had been given by their adoptive father in a tall linden, and Wilfred turned toward the west and Gottlieb toward the east.

First, we will follow Gottlieb for his name means *loved by God*.

4

After several years of wandering, as the animals grew and grew, Gottlieb arrived, with his lion, his bear, his wolf, his fox and his rabbit, at a large village which was completely draped in black.

He asked the first person he came upon where there might be an inn and the first person he came upon showed him the inn called the *Antlers of the Stag*.

He went therefore to the *Antlers of the Stag* and took a room for himself and a stable for his beasts, who had grown accustomed to living peacefully, each with the others, and sleeping on the same straw bed, as if they were all of the same species.

The innkeeper gave him a fine room, but for his animals the innkeeper had only a stable that was little more than a hole in the wall.

The rabbit went in first, because he had the most agile legs and because it was he who they usually sent as a scout. Now, it is also true, because he was the most timid and often fell victim to panicky fears, that he brought back the most absurd reports. So, this time, they also sent in the fox, who was so completely crafty and sharp that when he returned, rarely could they figure out whether to fear or to hope for what was out there.

This time the rabbit went straight to the food set out for them and brought back a cabbage.

The fox, going there in his turn, brought back a chicken.

The wolf, making himself as small as possible, followed the fox and brought back a sheep.

But the bear and the lion could not enter. So the innkeeper gave them an old cow, and they were able to eat their fill for three days.

When Gottlieb had provided for the maintenance of his beasts, which was always his first care, he asked the innkeeper why the village was draped in black.

"Because tomorrow," responded the innkeeper, "our king's daughter must die."

"Is she sick now?" asked the young man.

"No," answered the innkeeper. "On the contrary, she is young, fresh, and in quite good health, but she must die a most cruel death." And the innkeeper sighed.

"Why then must this be?" asked Gottlieb.

"Up high, on the mountain," answered the innkeeper, "there is a dragon with seven heads who, each year, devours a maiden; without which, he would devastate the country. Now only the daughter of the king remains, and, as there is no time left until the dragon begins his devastation, tomorrow the daughter of the king will be presented to it and after tomorrow she will be dead."

"But," asked the hunter, "Why has no one killed the dragon?"

"Alas," said the innkeeper, "many knights have already tried, and they have paid with their lives."

"Well," said Gottlieb, "All that you have told me is terrible indeed. Someone must save the princess."

So, Gottlieb went into the stable, assembled his council of beasts and sat, as president, on a stool.

When he had laid out the situation, the lion roared, the bear growled, the wolf howled, the fox reflected, and the rabbit trembled.

The lion said: "We must attack and tear it to pieces."

The bear said: "We must attack and smother it."

The wolf said: "Whatever the others will do, I will do also."

The fox said: "There must be a way to vanquish it without risking our skin."

The rabbit said: "My advice is that we must flee and the sooner the better."

The hunter said to the fox: "I will take your advice. Go and find out what's going on."

The fox left. Two hours later, he returned. He had consulted the oldest fox in the kingdom.

The old fox had said, "I would not know how to instruct your master on a means to vanquish the dragon, but there is, midway up the mountain road, a small chapel dedicated to St. Hubert, patron saint of hunters. Your master should go there and say his prayers this evening and spend the night there. Perhaps St. Hubert will see his devotion and inspire your master."

11

Gottlieb thanked the fox and decided to follow the advice from his old friend.

Night came, and without saying anything about his intentions, he left with his animals from the stable and set off toward the chapel.

Upon arriving, he knelt and said a prayer to the saint, while the animals sat respectfully behind.

His prayer completed, he lay down in a corner and fell asleep.

It was then that St. Hubert appeared to him, emanating a brilliant light.

"Tomorrow, upon arising," said the saint, "you will find on my altar three crystal chalices: one filled with wine red as ruby, another filled with wine white as topaz, the third and last filled with wine clear as diamond. Whoever drinks from these three chalices will untangle the riddle of the dragon."

When day broke, Gottlieb arose. His dream so completely held his thoughts that, when he opened his eyes, he immediately turned toward the altar.

On the altar, where the night before there had been nothing, he saw three chalices.

He approached the altar, took the ruby chalice and drank. As he returned it to the altar, he saw at the bottom of the cup the words, "He who has seven heads, has seven ways."

He then lifted the topaz chalice to his lips, drank from it, and read these words, "He who has seven ways, has seven wars."

He quickly raised the diamond chalice, drank it and read, "He who has seven wars, has seven sorrows. Your sword is under the lion."

He went quickly out of the chapel, nearly stepping on the lion asleep on the porch. Under the chapel porch he saw the tip of a great rock. He woke his animals.

"Raise this rock," he said to them.

The wolf, the fox and the rabbit rapidly dug around the rock. The bear and the lion were then able to raise it slowly to the porch.

Beneath the rock lay a shining silver saber. "A sword," he said to himself, "seven heads, seven ways, seven wars, seven sorrows: What does all this mean?"

But he cast aside his doubts. He knew that he had with him St. Hubert, patron saint of hunters. He and his beasts bravely climbed to the top of the mountain.

5

The hour had come to deliver the princess. The king with the marshal and the courtiers accompanied her to the foot of the mountain.

The princess continued on with the marshal until the chapel. There, the marshal remained to witness the sacrifice and bring back an account to the king.

The princess continued on, following the path to the summit, going with little will of her own, crying burning tears.

When she reached the top of the mountain, she was terribly afraid for she believed that the hunter and his five animals were nothing other than the dragon waiting to devour her.

But the hunter, quite the opposite, approached her respectfully, followed by his lion, his bear, his wolf, his fox and his rabbit, and, trying to put on the most agreeable face possible, saluted her and said, "Beautiful princess, do not at all fear me, and do not fear the animals who follow me. Very much the contrary, we have come to battle the dragon and deliver you."

"Good hunter," the princess said to him, "God give you aid, but I have no great hope. Many have already tried what you wish to attempt, and all have lost their lives."

"That may be," said the young hunter, still more encouraged by the marvelous beauty of the princess, "but whether we deliver you or we all lose our lives like they, the only real sadness would be to see the most beautiful princess in the world perish."

At that moment, a great storm approached from above. It was the dragon, flying and beating its wings. Then a cloud of smoke obscured the day, but this was nothing less than the breath of the monster.

"Go under that oak, princess," said Gottlieb, "and pray for your devoted servant."

The princess, trembling all over, went under the oak; the rabbit followed her. The other animals, that is to say, the lion, the bear, the wolf and the fox, stayed near their master.

All the while, the seven-headed dragon lowered itself, little by little, until it was twenty-five or thirty feet from the ground.

The hunter waited for it, the silver sword in his hand.

When the dragon saw Gottlieb, the dragon's first head said, "Why have you come to this mountain?" Then the second head said, "I wish you no harm," and the third head said, "Be gone!"

But Gottlieb responded to it, "While you may wish me no harm, I, myself, have sworn your death, for I have come to do battle with you. Defend yourself!"

"I never defend," said the fourth head, "I attack!" said the fifth.

And with these words it flew up into the clouds, so high that it seemed no larger than a swallow, and, throwing flame from the seven mouths of its seven heads, it let itself fall, as swiftly as lightening on the hunter, believing it could pluck him up in its claws and raise him into the air, as a falcon might seize a sparrow.

But Gottlieb, the lion, the bear, the wolf and the fox jumped away, forming a circle into which the dragon fell with a bump. "Oof," cried the sixth head. "You clumsy fool," said the seventh, and then the first retorted, "Clumsy? You ought to watch where you're going!"

And suddenly Gottlieb understood the words of the chalices. As the dragon beat its wings to rise and attack again, the hunter signaled to the bear and lion to grab its legs and hold them. He then told the wolf and the fox to run through brush, just out of the reach of the flames, crossing from one side to the other, passing each other, to distract the monster.

As the dragon struggled to rise, it saw the fox and wolf and leaned out to roast them and gobble them up, but the fox and the wolf were too quick. The fox called, "Come get me. I'm delicious broiled," and wolf howled, "Here, here! I make a very good stew. Ha! Ha!" And with the fox calling the pattern, they dashed back and forth, the heads following, blowing great yellow flames, bumping into each other, and getting tangled and twisted.

"Look out!" cried head one.

"Keep out of my way!" bellowed head two.

"Bah! Keep your flames to yourself!" muttered head three.

"Hey! Why don't you watch were you're going?" head four blurted out.

And then, finding themselves tied in a hopeless knot, heads five, six and seven said, "Oh dear! Now look what you've done. We can't move!"

Then the hunter ran up and pushed the tip of the sword just into the dragon's breast.

"Ouch!" cried head one.

"Ouch! Ouch!" yelled head two.

"Ouch! Ouch! Ouch!" screamed head three.

And head four said, "Don't do that!"

"It hurts!" head five said immediately after.

"That sword could kill us!" head six added.

"We give up!" head seven pled.

And Gottlieb replied, "But I must kill you to save the princess."

"No! No! No!" all seven heads said at once. "We were once seven sisters who lived by an enchanted forest and sold mushrooms in the village. One day in the forest, we were gathering our mushrooms when an evil woman changed us into this dragon. Some day you will find her and break this spell."

"But what about the maidens? Can I trust you? What will you eat?" Gottlieb questioned.

The seven heads replied, "As long as you possess that sword, we will harm no one."

And head one said, "We will have to eat grass."

But then head two said, "But I don't like grass. I shall eat holly."

And head three said, "Holly? You can't eat holly!"

And the hunter and his beasts, leaving the heads to squabble and untie themselves, walked away with the exception, of course, of the rabbit, who would no more dare to come near a tamed dragon than he would a wild one.

The combat finished, the hunter went to the beautiful princess, whom he found lying unconscious under the oak.

She had fainted from terror.

The rabbit was next to her, his eyes closed and, without the convulsive trembling that formerly agitated his whole body, appeared to have passed away.

Gottlieb went to a stream which ran nearby, took some water in the leaf of a water lily, and returned to shake some on the princess's face.

The cool spray woke the princess.

The hunter showed her the exhausted dragon and said, "You no longer have anything to fear, princess, you are delivered."

The princess began to thank St. Hubert who had given her liberator strength and courage. Then, turning to Gottlieb, she said, "Now, good hunter, you are going to be my beloved husband, because my father promised to make me the wife of any man who defeated the dragon."

And, in order to reward the animals, she removed her emerald necklace and fastened it around the lion's neck, her diamond earrings and put them on the ears of the bear, her pearl bracelet and passed it over the paw of the wolf and two priceless rings, one sapphire, the other ruby, which she gave to the fox and to the rabbit.

As for the hunter, she gave him her pocket handkerchief, still soaked with her tears, embroidered with her initials in gold.

The hunter then went to the dragon and asked permission to remove seven scales from each of the seven heads.

Head one said, "Of course, they grow back, eventually," and the other heads agreed. So the hunter slipped off the seven scales and put them in the handkerchief. The dragon returned to her cave to try and untie her knots.

6

After all this, the hunter was overwhelmed with fatigue and said to the princess, who was no less worn out from fear than he was fatigued from battle, "Princess, we are both so completely exhausted that we may not have the strength to go back down to the village. Let us sleep for a few moments."

She answered, "Yes, my dear hunter."

And both of them stretched out on the ground, side by side.

Only, just before falling asleep, the hunter said to the lion, "Lion, you are going to keep watch so that no one will attack us during our sleep. Understood?"

"Understood," said the lion.

The princess was already asleep.

The hunter then fell fast asleep as well.

The lion lay down near them, but, as he himself was very tired, he said to the bear, "Bear, would you be so kind as to keep watch in my place? I am so fatigued that I need to sleep a little. Only, at the least sign of danger, arouse me."

The bear lay down next to the lion. But he was himself so completely exhausted from the battle that he called to the wolf and said, "Wolf, you can see that I do not have the strength to keep my eyes open. Should something happen unexpectedly, wake me?"

The wolf lay down next to the bear, but his eyes kept closing despite his efforts. He motioned to the fox to come over.

"Fox," said he, "I am dying of sleep. Keep careful watch in my place and wake me at the least noise."

But the fox was so tired that he could not stand guard as he had been ordered. So, he called to the rabbit and said, "Rabbit, you even sleep with one eye open. I beg you to keep watch in my place. If you see anything that frightens you at all, awaken me.

But the poor rabbit had been so distressed by his own fears that, in fact, he was the most exhausted of them all. And so, he did what he had been told he must absolutely not do: he slept as deeply as all the others.

Thus, the hunter, the daughter of the king, the lion, the bear, the wolf, the fox and the rabbit were all profoundly asleep with no one keeping watch.

It was then that the marshal, who had stayed behind in the chapel to observe, not seeing the dragon carry off the daughter of the king, and noticing that all was quiet on the mountain, picked up his courage and crept up the mountain step by step, keeping his eyes open and his ears cocked, ready to flee at the least sign of danger.

Upon reaching the summit, the first thing he saw were the trees all burned and smoking, but the dragon had disappeared.

Then his eyes took him a little further.

He saw the daughter of the king, the hunter and the animals all plunged into the most profound sleep, and as the marshal was a man full of envy and ambition, he realized that he might just be able to pass himself off as the dragon-killer and marry the daughter of the king.

But to achieve this trick, he must first get rid of the true conqueror.

He took out his sword and approached Gottlieb so stealthily that not one animal awoke, not even the rabbit. Then bringing down his sword, he sliced off poor Gottlieb's head in a single cut.

He then woke the princess, who was very, very frightened, and he said to her, "You are in my hands, and I am going cut off your head, just as I did to the hunter, if you do not swear that you will say that it was I who killed the dragon."

"I cannot tell such a terrible lie," said the princess, "because it was the hunter and his animals who defeated the monster."

"You will nevertheless do as I wish," said the marshal, turning his bloody sword around the princess's head, "or I will cut you into pieces and say that the dragon did it."

The princess was so terribly frightened that she swore to do everything that the marshal wished.

Having obtained her oath, he took her to the king, who nearly died from the joy of seeing his dear daughter, whom he thought lost.

The marshal said to the king, "It is I who has killed the dragon and delivered not only the princess, but the empire as well. I ask, therefore, that she become my wife as you promised on your sacred word."

Since the marshal was not known as a man of courage, the king turned toward his daughter and said, "Is his story true?"

"Alas! Yes," said she, "it can only be true. Only, I insist that the marriage not take place for a year and a day." The marshal maintained that the marriage must be immediate, but the princess stood firm in her demand. So, the marshal, fearing if he pushed her too far that she might tell everything in a moment of despair, had to consent to the delay.

7

Ignorant of all this, the animals continued sleeping on the Mountain of the Dragon, around their master, who slept the sleep of the dead.

It was about an hour after the marshal had committed his crime and led away the princess that a very large bumblebee settled on the muzzle of the rabbit.

The rabbit, completely wrapped in sleep, passed his paw over his nose and chased away the pest.

But the bumblebee came a second time and sat down on the same spot.

The rabbit, still completely asleep, chased it away a second time.

Then the bumblebee came again a third time and, this time, not content to tickle the rabbit's nose with his feet, stung him with his stinger.

"Yeow," said the rabbit awakening.

Once awakened, the rabbit woke the fox, the fox woke the wolf, the wolf woke the bear, and the bear woke the lion.

But when the lion saw that the princess had gone and that his master's head was not connected to his body, he let out a terrible roar and cried, "Bear! What has happened? And why didn't you wake me?"

"Wolf! What has happened?" demanded the bear, "And why didn't you wake me?"

"Fox! What has happened?" demanded the wolf, "And why didn't you wake me?"

"Rabbit! What has happened?" demanded the fox, "And why didn't you wake me?"

And, as the rabbit had no one to question, he was certain that the anger of the other four animals would fall upon him. They all wanted to kill him, but he bowed his head sadly and said to them, "Don't kill me. I know a small wood up on a little hill where the root of life grows. A person who puts some of this root in his mouth is cured of all illnesses and all his wounds heal, and if his body is separated into two pieces, you only have to put some of this root in his mouth and put the two pieces together and they rejoin."

"And where is this wood?" asked the lion.

"Two hundred leagues from here," responded the rabbit.

"I will give you twenty-four hours to go and return," growled the lion. "Go now! And bring back a fat piece of that root."

The rabbit set off running with all his strength, and, at the end of twenty-four hours, he returned with a root the length and shape of a beet.

21

The lion said to the bear, "You who are so good with your paws, adjust the head of our master while I hold him up, so that the rabbit, standing on the shoulders of the wolf can place the root in his mouth."

The four animals went to work with a great passion because they loved their master with all their hearts, and they were filled with joy when the rabbit put the root of life in his master's mouth and his head re-joined his body, his heart began beating, and his life returned to him.

One fear remained, that the head would not stick. So the fox tickled Gottlieb's nose with the tip of his tail. Gottlieb sneezed and the head didn't budge. The operation had been a success!

Then the hunter asked his animals what had happened to the princess and what could possibly have kept them from noticing.

The animals told him what little they knew without hiding their error, and in the end, their devotion redeemed them.

All of a sudden, the rabbit cried out in terror, turned to the bear and said, "Clumsy beast! What have you done?"

The bear looked at Gottlieb and fell over backward.

He had re-connected the head, but in his fervor, he had put it on in reverse such that the hunter had his mouth facing back and the back of his head over his chest.

Luckily, the lion had ordered the rabbit to bring back a good-sized root, and the rabbit, as we have seen, had followed these orders.

The bear took the silver sword, which was as sharp as a razor, and sliced the air. The fox, who was as nimble as a monkey, helped the bear by guiding the blade along the line where the hunter had already been cut. The head came off neatly with the lion supporting it. And this time, with much greater care than the first, they replaced it properly. At which point, thanks to the root of life, the head reconnected immediately.

But afterward Gottlieb was sad, saying to the lion with a great sigh, "Why didn't you leave me in two pieces?" For he believed that the princess, in order to avoid marrying him, had cut off his head while he slept.

So, he set out to travel the world, showing his animals. People came running to see a lion with an emerald necklace, a bear with diamond earrings, a wolf with a pearl bracelet, and a fox and a rabbit, one with a ruby ring, the other with a ring of sapphire.

One day, after nearly a year had gone by, he and his beasts were passing by a dark forest very near the same village where he had saved the daughter of the king from the seven-headed dragon.

At the edge of the wood, he saw a doe as white as snow. As he was a true hunter at heart, he said to his beasts, "Let us chase this magnificent beast."

They pursued the white doe, not letting her out of sight, but never quite reaching her either. The chase had gone on for five hours, when, suddenly, the doe disappeared like smoke.

Only then did he realize that he had gone well into the forest. With night falling, he resolved to stay in the forest until the next morning, thinking that now it would be impossible to find the way out. He then lit a fire at the foot of a tree and set up camp.

When nothing was visible, except by the dancing rays of light from the fire, he, along with his beasts, stretched out next to the flames. Then he thought he heard something like a human voice crying. He looked all around him but could not see a living soul.

A second moan made itself heard. He was certain that it was coming from above.

Gottlieb raised his head. Looking up, he saw an old woman perched high in a tree.

"Hou, hou, hou!" said the old woman. "Hou, hou, hou! that I am cold."

The young hunter looked at her with astonishment and, although she seemed more like an owl than a woman, he took pity on her.

"If you are as cold as all that, mother," he said to her, "come down and warm yourself."

"No," answered the old woman, "your beasts will bite me."

Then she repeated, "Hou, hou, hou! I am freezing here."

"My beasts have never harmed anyone," answered Gottlieb. "Do not fear them at all and come sit near my fire."

But the old woman, who was really a witch, said to him, "No, I am too afraid. I will not come down, at least not unless you would touch the backs of your animals with the branch that I am going to throw you. In that case, I will come down."

Gottlieb began to laugh and as he could see no harm in doing what the old woman asked, and, moreover, taking her to be quite mad, answered, "Break your branch. Send it to me and I will touch the backs of my animals."

He had no sooner repeated those words, when the branch fell at his feet.

He picked it up without suspecting anything and touched his animals, who, at this contact, became completely still. They had changed to stone.

While Gottlieb looked with stupefaction at the phenomenon that had just occurred, the old woman slid down the trunk of the tree, and, coming up behind him, touched her wand to the young hunter, who became in an instant as petrified as his animals.

Then she carted him and his five animals into a cave, where there were many other poor people changed into stone by her evil spells.

9

As all this was going on, right at that moment by chance, Wilfred, who had gone to the west, was standing under a silver birch. He had searched for an opportunity to serve as a hunter but had found nothing. He then had led his dancing beasts to markets and carnivals.

Under the silver birch he heard a voice and looked up. There the bird of gold was saying to him, "You must return now. You must consult the knife in the linden tree." And then she was gone.

He and his beasts immediately set off for the kingdom and the tree. They walked all day and as much of the night as they could, until they came to the tree of separation. Upon reaching it, he saw that the blade was shiny on the side from which he came, but rusty on the side facing where his brother had gone.

He became frightened. Yet, it was only half rusty, and he said to himself, "Something terrible has happened to my brother, but perhaps I can still aid him, because half of the blade is still clear."

Without wasting a minute, he set off on the road to the east and the bird of gold again appeared and led him to the edge of the enchanted forest and said, "Here you will find your brother."

The bird of gold then flew over the same white doe that his brother had seen and was gone. So, like his brother, he entered the forest, followed by his beasts, and pursued the doe without ever being able to catch her, until she disappeared just as he thought he had her trapped. With night falling, he found himself forced, like his brother, to set up camp in the wood.

Having, like his brother, lit a fire, he heard moaning coming from somewhere above his head.

"Ayee! Ayee! Ayee!" said a voice, "that it is cold here!"

He raised his head and saw the old witch with her eyes like an owl.

"If you are cold up there, good mother," he said to her, "come down and warm yourself."

"I remain," answered the witch. "Your beasts would eat me."

"My beasts are not mean. They will do nothing to you. Come down!"

"I am going to throw down a stick," said she, "and, indeed, if you tap them with this stick they will do nothing to me."

On hearing these words, the hunter was a bit taken back and said, "What I said about my beasts will have to be enough for you. Come down, otherwise I'm going up there and bring you down."

"Bah!" said the old woman. "Come and get me! You couldn't do it if you wanted to!"

"We will see about that," said the hunter, "and to begin, I'm going to send you an arrow."

"I laugh at your arrows," said the witch. "Try it, and you will see."

The hunter pulled back his bowstring and sent an arrow flying.

But, when it came to ordinary arrows, the witch was immune.

"You aren't much of a shot!" cackled the witch and threw back his arrow.

Seeing that he had been checked, the hunter, who seldom wasted a shot, had no doubt what his business was with this old woman.

So, he tried another means. Stringing the silver arrow the old hunter had given him, he drew and sent it forth, and, as the witch was not safe from arrows of silver, he struck her in the thigh so perfectly that she came tumbling down from the top of the tree to the bottom.

The hunter set his foot on her chest and said, "You old hag, if you do not tell me this instant what you have done with my brother, I'm going to pick you up and throw you into the fire."

She became very frightened and begged for mercy.

"Where is my brother?" the hunter demanded with even greater insistence.

"Your brother is in a cave," she answered, "He is changed to stone: he and his beasts."

He forced the witch to lead him to the cave, making her hop on one leg. When they had arrived, "Now, old witch," said he, "you are going to bring not only my brother and his beasts back to life, but all the petrified people here."

The witch, seeing that she had to obey, took her wand and touched each stone and the young hunter and his beasts got up, as well as an entire crowd of people: travelers, merchants, artisans, soldiers. Each of whom warmly thanked their liberator and set off, each to his own home.

As soon as the brothers saw each other they jumped into each others' arms, rejoicing with all their hearts to be so miraculously brought together.

18

Then Gottlieb told Wilfred about the dragon, the battle, the princess and his disappointment. And Wilfred said, "Take heart. You must return to the village. Such a princess could never have been so cruel."

So, they tied the old woman to her cart, broke her wand, tended her wound, and asked the two bears to pull her through the forest. Gottlieb led the way, while Wilfred fell asleep on the back of his faithful lion.

By sunrise they had reached the edge of the forest where they happened upon a small cabin. The door was open and the two brothers entered.

On the table were seven plates with seven forks, seven spoons, seven knives and seven cups. In the room behind, there were seven beds.

"Stay here," Gottlieb said to his brother. "I know who lives here and these dear people will not be returning for some time. Keep the old woman tied. I will send for you tomorrow." It was exactly one year since he had battled the dragon.

Gottlieb and his beasts then set off for the village and the castle of the king and his daughter.

This time, when they arrived, the entire village was draped in scarlet.

He asked his innkeeper, "What is the meaning of this? A year ago, the whole village was draped in black. Today, everything is red."

The innkeeper responded, "Do you recall that a year ago the daughter of the king was to be sent to the dragon?"

"Perfectly," said Gottlieb.

"Well, the marshal battled and vanquished the monster, and, tomorrow, we are going to celebrate his marriage to the daughter of the king. That's why, a year ago, the village was in mourning and why, today, it is festive."

The next day, the day of the wedding, the hunter said to the innkeeper, "Would you like, my dear host, to bet with me that today I will eat the king's bread, taken right from his table?"

"I will bet you one hundred pieces of gold that you will do no such a thing," responded the innkeeper.

The hunter took the bet and set down a sack containing the amount of the wager. Then he called the rabbit and said, "My dear little runner, go quickly and bring me some of the bread the king intends to eat."

Because the rabbit was the smallest and least important member of the troupe, he could not refuse this commission and immediately set out.

"Aye, aye," thought the rabbit, "when I go out all alone and run down the village streets, all the neighborhood dogs are going to be hot on my heels as soon as I pass by."

And sure enough, at the end of five minutes, he had as a tail a veritable pack of dogs of every species whose clear intention was to have him for lunch.

But he ran and jumped so well that you could hardly see him go by. Finally, pushed to the limit, he slid into a guardhouse so adroitly that the guard on duty didn't notice that he was no longer alone.

The dogs wished to follow him there, but the guard didn't know what this pack wanted and, believing they were after him, doled out several strong blows with the butt of his staff and poked at them with his halberd.

The dogs fled howling.

As soon as the rabbit saw that the coast was clear, he jumped out of the guardhouse, to the great astonishment of the guard, and in one jump arrived at the palace. He went straight to the princess and, sliding under her chair, softly scratched her foot.

The princess thought that it was her little lapdog, and because she was in no mood to be bothered, said, "Go away, Phoenix! Get out of here!"

But the rabbit scratched again, and princess said again, "Do you want me to throw you out, Phoenix?"

But the rabbit continued to scratch. Finally, the princess leaned over and looked.

The rabbit showed her his paw with her ring.

The princess recognized the rubies that she had given to the rabbit of her liberator. She hugged the rabbit to her chest and carried him to her room.

"Dear little rabbit," she asked, "what do you wish of me?"

"My master, he who defeated the dragon, is here," said he "and has sent me to bring back some of the king's bread."

Overjoyed, the princess called for the royal baker and ordered him to return with some of the king's bread.

"But it is also necessary," said the rabbit, "that the baker carry me to my master's inn so that the dogs don't eat my bread and me with it."

At the door of the inn, the little rabbit took the bread between his front paws, stood up on his hind paws, and, hopping carefully, carried the bread to his master.

"You see, my host," said the hunter, "the one hundred pieces of gold are mine. Here is the king's bread and the proof can be seen by the coat of arms carved upon it."

The innkeeper was completely astonished, but his astonishment doubled when he heard the hunter add, "I have the king's bread. That is all well and good, but now I wish to have the king's roast beef."

"Ah! I would certainly like to see that!" said the innkeeper. "Only, I will no longer bet."

Gottlieb called his fox and said, "My dear little fox, go quickly and bring back a bit of the roast beef that the king intends to eat."

Mr. Fox wished to outshine his friend the rabbit. He dashed out to the road, and slipped down the backstreets so craftily that not one dog saw him. As the rabbit had done, he entered the palace, and as the rabbit had also done, he hid beneath the chair of the king's daughter and scratched her foot.

She leaned over and looked. Between the legs of the chair, the fox stuck out his paw with the sapphire ring given him by the princess.

Immediately, the princess carried him into her room, where, as soon as she entered, she asked, "My dear fox, what do you wish of me?"

"My master," said the fox, "he who defeated the dragon, is here, and sent me to humbly request that you give me some of the king's roast beef."

She called for the royal cook and ordered him to put the fox and a piece of the king's roast beef in a basket and carry them both to the inn. These orders were punctually executed. There, the fox took the plate from the hands of the royal cook and, chasing away the flies with his tail, carried it to Gottlieb.

"Well, well, my host," said the hunter. "Here are the bread and the roast beef. Now I am going to send for some of the king's vegetables."

Calling then the wolf, he said, "My good little wolf, go quickly to the palace and bring back to me some of the vegetables that the king intends to eat."

The wolf ran straight to the palace, because he had no fear of being attacked. He went to the princess's room and, pulling on her dress, caused her to turn around. She recognized his pearl bracelet and stroked his head. Since she was alone, she said, "My dear little wolf, what is it that you wish?"

"My master," answered the wolf, "he who defeated the dragon, has requested that I ask you for some of the king's vegetables."

She once again called for the royal cook and commanded him to take some of the king's vegetables to the inn.

The cook set off, followed by the wolf like a pet dog. At the door of the inn, he gave the plate to the wolf, who carried it to his master.

"You see, my dear host," said Gottlieb, "We have here already the king's bread, the king's roast beef, and the king's vegetables, but my dinner would be incomplete if I did not get the king's dessert."

And, calling to his bear, "My little bear," said he, "so well acquainted are you with honey, chocolate and cake, go to the palace and bring back some of the best desserts that the king intends to eat."

The bear sauntered out, hiding even less than the wolf; for, far from being nervous about being seen, he made everyone else flee as he passed.

In front of the palace door, the guard, crossing his bayonet in front of him, refused to allow the bear to enter. Then, since the bear kept insisting and growling, the guard called the rest of the company.

But the bear stood up on his hind feet and distributed so many vigorous punches with his right and his left that all the soldiers were sent rolling head-over-heels to the ground. The bear then strode calmly into the palace. Seeing the princess, he sat behind her and very, very gently growled.

Hearing his growls, she turned around and, having heard those growls before, recognized the bear by his diamond earrings.

She led him into her room and said to him, "My gentle, little bear, what do you wish of me?"

"My master," said the bear, "he who defeated the dragon, sent me here to beg you to give me some desserts from the table of the king."

She called for the royal confectioner and ordered him to carry a plate covered with desserts from the table of the king to the door of the inn.

Arriving there, the bear commenced with the tip of his tongue to gather up all the bonbons that had accidentally fallen to the ground and, standing up, took the platter and carried it to his master.

"Aha! Mr. Innkeeper," said Gottlieb, "the delicacies have arrived. I have thus the bread, the roast beef, the vegetables, and the dessert from the table of the king. Now, I should have some of the king's wine, because I would not know how to eat all these good things without something to drink."

12

He called then to his lion and said, "My good little lion, go to the palace and bring back some of the very wine the king drinks at his table."

The lion set off immediately for the palace. At the sight of him, every single person ran for his life. The merchants closed their shops and shut their doors. When the lion appeared in front of the palace, the entire post took up arms and tried to prevent the lion from entering, but with just one roar, the lion sent them all fleeing.

Thus, he entered the palace freely, came to the door of the king's daughter, and knocked with his tail. When the princess came to open the door, she was so frightened at first that she jumped back. But then she recognized the emerald necklace around his neck. She asked him in, and said, "My dear lion, what do you wish?"

"My master," answered the lion, "he who defeated the dragon, sent me to you to most humbly request some of the wine that the king drinks."

The princess called for the royal wine master and told him to go to the wine cellar and take several bottles of the king's wine to the inn.

The wine master began to go down into the wine cellar, but the lion said, "One moment, sommelier, my friend. I am acquainted with people of your sort, and I will go with you to the cellar to see what you are giving me."

He followed the wine master into the cellar. There, the wine master, believing he could easily fool the lion, began to pull off the racks some of the wine reserved for the servants.

"Stop right there, comrade! It is necessary that I dignify the confidence that my master has in me. I must taste the wine before bringing it to him."

He poured out a half-bottle and swallowed it in one gulp. "Aha!" he said, shaking his head. "Are you trying to be humorous? Another wine! And step lively! This one can be served to the servants, at best."

The wine master looked askance at the lion, but held his tongue. He led the lion to another cask, reserved for the king's marshal.

But the lion said to him, "Stop right there! I must taste it."

He poured another half-bottle and drank it in one gulp. He clicked his tongue and, a little more satisfied, said, "It is better than the other, but it is still not right."

The wine master, now getting quite angry, said under his breath, "How can an animal as stupid as you understand wine?"

But before he could finish these words, the lion smacked him with his tail and sent him rolling to the other end of the cellar.

The wine master picked himself up and, without breathing another word, led the lion to a small room in the cellar where the wine reserved for his majesty was kept. No one else in the kingdom was ever allowed to drink this wine.

The lion, after drinking a half bottle as a taste, shook his head up and down as a sign of satisfaction, and said, "Yes, finally, this is the proper wine."

He then filled six bottles. After that, he went back up the stairs, followed by the wine master, but when he reached the courtyard, he began to weave side to side so much that the wine master was obliged to carry the basket to the inn, fearing that the lion might break the bottles or allow them to be stolen.

There the wine master hung the basket from the lion's mouth, and the lion carried it to his master.

Then the hunter said, "You see, Mr. Innkeeper, I have the bread, the wine, the roast beef, the vegetables and the dessert from the king's table. I am now going to eat like a king with my beasts."

And, this said, he sat at the table, giving to the lion, to the bear, to the wolf, to the fox, and to the rabbit, their shares of the dinner. He ate well and drank well and was in fine humor, because he could see, by how quickly she fulfilled his wishes, that the princess loved him still.

That night he slept with great contentment.

13

The next afternoon, he said to the innkeeper, "Mr. Innkeeper, now that I have eaten and drunk what the king eats and drinks, I wish to go to the palace and marry the daughter of the king."

"How could you do a thing like that?" asked the innkeeper. "The princess is already engaged, and this same day the marriage must be celebrated."

Then the hunter pulled from his pocket the princess's handkerchief, which held the seven scales of the dragon.

"What I hold within this cloth," said he to the innkeeper, "will assist me in my project, as insane as it may seem to you."

The innkeeper opened his eyes wide and said, "I believe quite willingly everything that you tell me, but as for wedding the daughter of the king, I will wager my house and my garden that you will not."

The hunter took a sack containing one thousand pieces of gold and said, "Here is my stake against your property."

While all this was going on at the inn, the king, seated for dinner, said to his daughter, "What do you want with all these beasts who are coming to you, entering my palace and then leaving?"

"I cannot say," said the princess, "but send for their master. You will do well."

The king immediately sent one of his servants to tell the hunter to come to the palace. The servant arrived at the inn just as the hunter was concluding his bet with the innkeeper.

"Well, well, my dear host, the king has sent one of his servants to invite me to go see him, but I am not going to the king so easily."

And, turning to the messenger, "Return and tell the king," said he, "that he should wish to do me honor by sending me proper attire for the festival, a carriage with six horses, and an escort.

When this response was transmitted by the messenger to the king, he asked his daughter, "What must I do?"

"Do what he asks of you," she responded, "and you will do well."

So the king sent to the hunter fine clothes for the festival, a carriage pulled by six horses, and an escort.

When Gottlieb saw the royal carriage, "Well, well, my host," said he, "they have sent me all that I desired."

And he put on the fine clothes, and called the fox. "Fox, go to the mountain. You know what you must do."

The fox winked and left the inn running as swiftly as the wind.

The hunter then called the wolf. "Wolf, go to my brother. Show him and our old friend to the castle."

The wolf was out the door in a single bound and raced away.

The hunter then put on his sword, climbed into the carriage with the remaining animals, and went off to the palace.

When the king saw him come, he said to his daughter, "How must I receive him?"

"Go before him, my father," said the princess, "and you will do well."

The king went therefore up to the hunter and led him, the lion, the bear and the rabbit into the palace.

All the grand people of the kingdom were assembled in the great open courtyard of the palace and the king seated the hunter between the king himself and his daughter, facing the marshal. But the marshal did not recognize him, although he had once cut off his head.

Then they brought out, for all the guests to see, the burned branches and trunks from the mountain.

The king said, "This is all that remains of the dragon that the marshal killed. That is why, today, I am giving him my daughter in marriage."

Then the hunter stood up, untied the kerchief and said, "Not quite. These seven scales remain of the dragon." The marshal turned pale and stammered, "D-d-dragons h-have s-scales?"

The hunter looked at the marshal and said, "They do and these are the true scales of the dragon, testimony to the triumph of the victor."

Then, shaking the handkerchief, he asked the princess if she recalled giving it to someone.

"I gave it to the one who defeated the dragon," answered the princess.

At that moment, the sky became so dark that it seemed a thunderstorm was about to break. The people looked up and screamed and ran under the arches of the walls.

Then, the dragon, with the fox riding her back, slowly floated down from the sky, little puffs of smoke coming from the fourteen nostrils of the seven heads. She landed in the middle of the courtyard and the fox leaped from her back. The people cowered under the arches.

Then Gottlieb said, "Dragon, do you recognize these scales?"

And the seven heads replied, "Oh, quite. They were removed by the one who has the sword that subjugates us."

Just then the wolf led in a man who looked exactly like Gottlieb, leading a lion, a bear, a wolf, a fox, a rabbit, and an old woman, tied to a cart. And all the grand people could only stare and stare.

Then Gottlieb said, "Dragon, would you be so kind as to re-light these charred branches and trunks. I need a fire."

And head one said, "As you wish."

Then with a great burst of flame, the dragon began a bonfire with the marshal's supposed evidence.

Suddenly, to the shock and amazement of all the people, the two brothers took the witch and threw her into the flames, but the instant the flames touched her, she rolled back. Suddenly, her face lost its wrinkles. Her back became straight. Her hair turned a lovely auburn, and she said, "Well, it was about time you threw me into the fire. That was the only way to break the spell on me. You see, I was the marshal's mother, until I used the wrong book of recipes to make porridge and turned myself into a witch."

And as everyone's eyes returned to the center of the courtyard, the dragon disappeared into smoke and in her place stood seven lovely sisters.

Then the hunter called his lion and took off his emerald necklace; his bear and took off his diamond earrings; his wolf and took off his pearl bracelet; his fox and his rabbit and took off their rings.

He then showed these jewels to the princess. "Do you recognize these jewels," he asked her.

"Certainly," answered the princess, "for I am the one who shared them among the animals who helped the one who defeated the dragon in his battle."

"And who is this 'one who defeated the dragon'?" asked Gottlieb finally.

"You are the one," answered the princess.

"But how," demanded the king, "is it that you have never boasted of your victory or claimed the hand of my daughter?"

"Because I was fatigued from the battle, I lay down and slept," replied Gottlieb. "Then the marshal came and cut off my head. He then forced the princess to name him the dragon killer. But truth triumphs!

Then, since several doubters were astonished that someone who had lost his head to the marshal carried himself so well, he recounted the way that the animals had brought him back to life, how he had traveled the world with them for a year, and how finally he had learned from the innkeeper of the treachery of the marshal.

Then the king asked his daughter "Is it true that this young man is the one who defeated the dragon?"

"Yes, it is true," she answered. "I had sworn—I was forced into my silence. But today, without my collaboration, the villainy of the marshal has been shown to all. Only then did I speak. Yes," she added, pointing to Gottlieb, "yes, here is the conqueror of the dragon. It is good that I gave him my handkerchief, and it is good that I gave his animals my jewels. That is why I asked that a year and a day pass before I married the marshal, hoping that, in the space of a year and a day, the truth would show itself.

44

Then the king called together his council of twelve to judge the marshal. They condemned him to live with his mother and be demoted to a court jester.

The judgment was executed to the great satisfaction of the king's subjects who detested the marshal. Unfortunately, he was not a very good jester. He could never make anyone laugh, except his mother, who laughed a great deal now that she wasn't a witch.

The king gave his daughter in marriage to the hunter and immediately named him governor general of the entire kingdom.

The vows were then celebrated with great magnificence, and at the wedding dinner, the young governor remembered his father and his adoptive father and asked them to come live in the village near him.

He didn't forget the innkeeper either, and, calling him to the table, said, "Ah well, my host, here it is that I have wed the daughter of the king, and, as a result, your house and your garden belong to me."

"Yes," said the innkeeper. "It is in accordance with justice."

"No," said the young governor. "It will be in accordance with clemency. Keep your house and your garden, and throw the thousand pieces of gold into the bargain."

On his right sat the princess, her father and his animals. On his left sat his brother, the seven sisters, and his animals.

He turned to his brother and said, "You may now, if you wish, marry one of these beautiful sisters that we have saved from their curse as a dragon. We shall share this beautiful kingdom."

Hearing these words, the first sister said, "It shall be me. I am the first."

"No," said the second, "I am the most beautiful."

"Hardly," said the third, "No one has either my looks or my charm."

And Gottlieb looked at Wilfred and said, "One day, I shall tell you about the seven wars and the seven sorrows," and they both laughed as the bird of gold came and settled on Wilfred's shoulder, and they and their animals never parted again.

About the Translator:

Nathan Dickmeyer grew up in Michigan and has degrees from Michigan State, Harvard and Stanford Universities. He has also studied Persian at Columbia University. From his website, www.dickmeyerconsulting.com, one can download vocabulary-building spreadsheets for French, Persian, Chinese and English. He lives in Nyack, New York.

About the Illustrator:

Roya Sadeghi is a native of Iran and is a graduate of Al-Zahra University in Mathematics. She has studied painting with Master Aydin Aghdashloo. Roya has illustrated several children's books and is currently an instructor of painting to children. She lives in Tehran, Iran.